MW00981952

Tiger Roars

Written and illustrated by

Wang Zumin and **Wang Ying**

CARDINAL
MEDIA

I am tiger and I do whatever I want.

I wrestle Howie the lion for his toy.

I grab Tommy the bear's tricycle.

I knock over the block tower that Fifi the elephant and Charlie the crocodile built.

Today is my birthday. My mom brought a big cake for me to share with everyone.

But nobody wants to celebrate with me...

Kiki the rabbit tells me I'm not nice.

Kiki is right. I haven't been nice.

I let out a roar and say,
"I'm sorry, everyone!
I'm sorry I wasn't nice."

Kiki the rabbit asks, "Do you promise you'll be nicer?"

"I promise. I'm sorry I was mean
to everyone," I say.

Kiki gives me a hug. "Thank you," I say.

Kiki whispers to me, "How about we share some of your birthday cake now?"

It's fun to have friends.

ISBN 978-1-64074-049-5

Printed in China
2 4 6 8 10 9 7 5 3 1

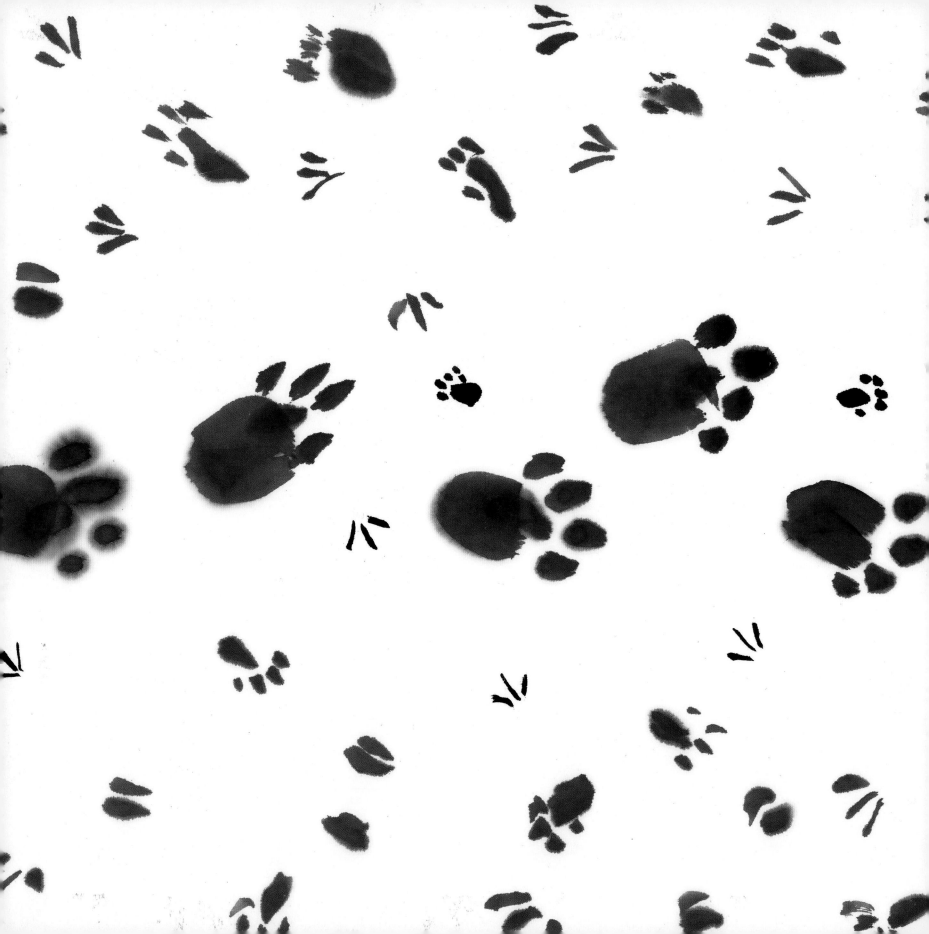